Dear Parent:
Your child's love of reading starts here!

Every child learns to read in a different way and at his or her own speed. Some go back and forth between reading levels and read favorite books again and again. Others read through each level in order. You can help your young reader improve and become more confident by encouraging his or her own interests and abilities. From books your child reads with you to the first books he or she reads alone, there are I Can Read Books for every stage of reading:

SHARED READING
Basic language, word repetition, and whimsical illustrations, ideal for sharing with your emergent reader

BEGINNING READING
Short sentences, familiar words, and simple concepts for children eager to read on their own

READING WITH HELP
Engaging stories, longer sentences, and language play for developing readers

READING ALONE
Complex plots, challenging vocabulary, and high-interest topics for the independent reader

ADVANCED READING
Short paragraphs, chapters, and exciting themes for the perfect bridge to chapter books

I Can Read Books have introduced children to the joy of reading since 1957. Featuring award-winning authors and illustrators and a fabulous cast of beloved characters, I Can Read Books set the standard for beginning readers.

A lifetime of discovery begins with the magical words "I Can Read!"

Visit www.icanread.com for information
on enriching your child's reading experience.

Leaf it to Fiona!
—H. P.

For Bunny and Paris
—L. A.

Gouache and black pencil were used to prepare the full-color art.

I Can Read Book® is a trademark of HarperCollins Publishers.

Amelia Bedelia is a registered trademark of Peppermint Partners, LLC.

Library of Congress Cataloging-in-Publication Data

Parish, Herman.

Amelia Bedelia hits the trail / by Herman Parish ; illustrated by Lynne Avril.

    p. cm.—(I can read! 1-beginning reading)

"Greenwillow Books."

Summary: On a nature hike with her class, young Amelia Bedelia's literal-mindedness causes confusion along with some laughs.

ISBN 978-0-06-209527-5 (hardback)—ISBN 978-0-06-209526-8 (pbk.) [1. Hiking—Fiction. 2. Nature study—Fiction. 3. School field trips—Fiction. 4. Humorous stories.] I. Avril, Lynne, (date) illustrator. II. Title. PZ7.P2185Aon 2013 [E]—dc23 2012036841

16 17 18 PC/WOR 10 9 8 7 6 5 4 3   First Edition

Greenwillow Books

I Can Read!

BEGINNING
1
READING

Amelia Bedelia
·Hits the Trail·

by **Herman Parish** ❀ pictures by **Lynne Avril**

Greenwillow Books, *An Imprint of* HarperCollins*Publishers*

Amelia Bedelia was going hiking.

Her entire class was going, too.

"Let's hit the trail," said Miss Edwards,

Amelia Bedelia's teacher.

5

The trail was steep.

Everyone stepped over a big tree root.

Amelia Bedelia was chatting

and looking up at the birds and . . .

SPLAT!!

Amelia Bedelia fell flat on her face.

"Are you okay?" asked Miss Edwards.

"I'm okay," said Amelia Bedelia.

"But the next time I hit the trail,

I'll use this stick instead of my face!"

Amelia Bedelia and her friends
spotted lots of living things
along the trail.

They saw a deer
and a rabbit.

They saw squirrels
and chipmunks.

They saw insects
crawling along the ground

and flying in the air.

Birds chirped
in the trees.

When a snake crossed the trail,
Chip let out a yell.

"Relax," said Penny.
"It is more scared of you
than you are of it."

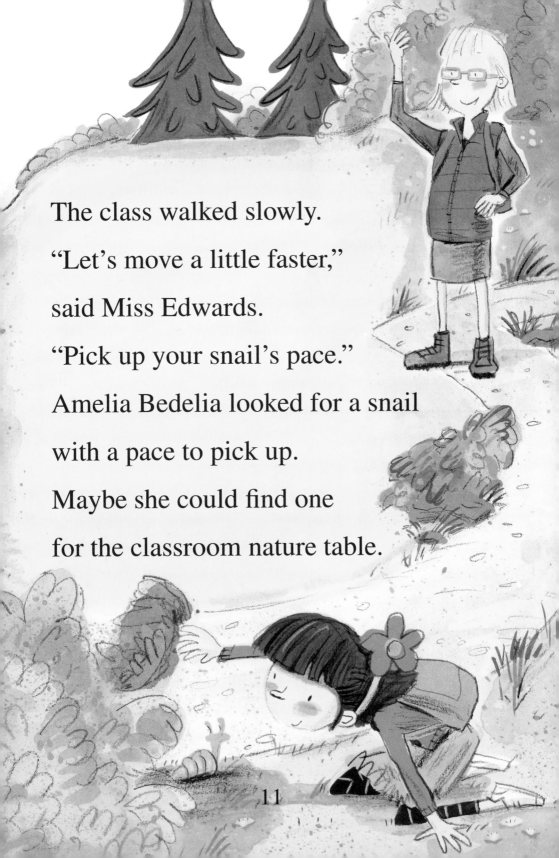

The class walked slowly.

"Let's move a little faster,"

said Miss Edwards.

"Pick up your snail's pace."

Amelia Bedelia looked for a snail

with a pace to pick up.

Maybe she could find one

for the classroom nature table.

11

"I'm hungry," said Clay.

"Can we eat lunch?"

Miss Edwards read her map.

"There is a stream ahead," she said.

"We can stop there for a bite."

"I have lots of bites," said Amelia Bedelia.

"I can see water!" said Penny.

The class raced to the stream.

14

"We'll eat lunch on the bank.

Dig in!" said Miss Edwards.

Amelia Bedelia
didn't see a bank,

or even a cash machine.

Was there treasure buried here?
Why else would Miss Edwards tell them
to dig in?

It was time to go back to school.

Wade was the last to finish his lunch.

"Let's go, Wade," said Miss Edwards.

"Yay!" said Amelia Bedelia.

Amelia Bedelia took off
her shoes and socks
and waded right into the stream.

Soon everyone was splashing

with Amelia Bedelia.

Even Miss Edwards joined the fun.

As they walked back,
everyone found things
for the nature table.

Daisy picked a daisy.

Holly plucked
a sprig of holly.

Rose found
a wild rose.

Amelia Bedelia
picked up fallen leaves.

20

"What did you find, Amelia Bedelia?"

asked Miss Edwards.

"These are my leafs," said Amelia Bedelia.

Miss Edwards smiled.

"When you have more than one leaf,

you say *leaves*," she said.

That made sense to Amelia Bedelia.

In the fall, every leaf

had to leave its tree.

Amelia Bedelia knew

she would not think anymore

of a leaf falling off a tree.

She would think

it was leaving

its tree.

"Nice leaves," said Skip.

"You have maple,

oak,

and chestnut," he said.

Skip knew a lot about trees.
"What is this red one?"
asked Amelia Bedelia.

"Uh-oh," said Skip. "That is poison ivy!"

Amelia Bedelia threw the leaves

up in the air.

Her leaves were leaving again!

Skip laughed so hard
he fell on the ground.
"I was joking!" he said.
Amelia Bedelia was not laughing.
"That was a mean trick," she said.

"Maybe you should take a hike,"
said Skip.

"I am," said Amelia Bedelia.

"And now I don't have anything
for the nature table."

Amelia Bedelia's lip trembled.

"I'm sorry, Amelia Bedelia," said Skip.

He helped Amelia Bedelia

pick up her leaves.

"Hold still!" Skip said.

"Are you teasing again?"

asked Amelia Bedelia.

"No. You have a hitchhiker," said Skip.

He pointed at a caterpillar.

The caterpillar was crawling

on Amelia Bedelia's backpack.

"Wow!" said Amelia Bedelia.

Amelia Bedelia's caterpillar

was the star of the nature table.

Then it was the star

of Amelia Bedelia's classroom . . .

30

until it hit the trail.